I See the Winds

I See the Winds

BY KAZUE MIZUMURA

Thomas Y. Crowell Company NEW YORK

Manufactured in the United States of America
Library of Congress Catalog Card No. 66-12670
1 2 3 4 5 6 7 8 9 10

To E. M. R.

Once again
the wind rustled the young leaves
and the trees turned
to greet spring.

Waiting for the children,
the wind pushes empty swings
in the spring rain.

Wind, wind,
there's no place to hide
in the blue sky.
Come blow my kite.

May wind is busy
Brushing the robin's tail,
Combing the willow tree,
And whispering to my ear
that summer is near.

I may be a boy
but call me a man
hauling the sails
on this very summer day.

Chasing the fireflies,
I caught
only the cool summer breeze.

Gently, gently, the wind blows
dandelions' parachutes
into the afternoon sun.

A lone gull
Daring the angry wind
Swings back and forth
above the swelling sea.

In the evening glow
the wind gathers
the chattering birds.
It is time to go to bed.

Cat's whiskers
faintly quivered
in the slanted shadow—
summer is gone.

I see the wind
on the tree tops
tinkling gold spangled leaves
against the sky so high.

From a mountain of fallen leaves
totters a pheasant:
A windy night last night.

Raging wind
whipped foaming horses.
Phantom chariots
thunder over the sea.

In the northwest wind
dry weeds sob.
Tomorrow will be snow.

Snowflakes drift.
I taste winter
melting on my lips.

Huddled starlings
on the winter branch
Sway with the wind
Have no song.

While the last wind of winter
persuades the snow to linger
The crocuses call for spring.

ABOUT THE AUTHOR-ILLUSTRATOR

KAZUE MIZUMURA is well known as an illustrator and jacket artist for both children's and adult books. Her busy life also includes textile design, advertising layout, and Japanese brush drawing.

Miss Mizumura was born in Kamakura, Japan. She studied at the Women's Art Institute in Tokyo, as well as at Pratt Institute in Brooklyn, New York. Miss Mizumura now lives in Stamford, Connecticut.